To Valerie—With love and appreciation for all that you did.
FJS

To Bryan. Always have, always will.
KLP

First published in Great Britain in 2023 by Jessica Kingsley Publishers
An imprint of Hodder & Stoughton Ltd
An Hachette Company

1

Copyright © Frank J. Sileo and Kate Lum-Potvin 2023

The right of Frank J. Sileo and Kate Lum-Potvin to be identified as the
Authors of the Work has been asserted by them in accordance with
the Copyright, Designs and Patents Act 1988.

Illustrations copyright © Emmi Smid 2023
Foreword copyright © Vanessa Williams 2023

Front cover image source: Emmi Smid

A CIP catalogue record for this title is available from
the British Library and the Library of Congress

ISBN 978 1 83997 526 4
eISBN 978 1 83997 527 1

Printed and bound in China by Leo Paper Products Ltd

Jessica Kingsley Publishers' policy is to use papers that are
natural, renewable and recyclable products and made from wood
grown in sustainable forests. The logging and manufacturing
processes are expected to conform to the environmental
regulations of the country of origin.

Jessica Kingsley Publishers
Carmelite House
50 Victoria Embankment
London EC4Y 0DZ

www.jkp.com

PRIDE
AND
JOY

A Story About
Becoming an
LGBTQIA+ Ally

Foreword by Vanessa Williams
Illustrated by Emmi Smid

Frank J. Sileo
and
Kate Lum-Potvin

Jessica Kingsley Publishers
London and Philadelphia

Foreword by Vanessa Williams

"Careful the things you say...children will listen." I had the pleasure of singing those powerful words when I starred as the Witch in the Broadway musical "Into the Woods" in 2002, written by the incomparable Stephen Sondheim.

That message about how impressionable young children are should remind adults and the world at large to always lead with love, demonstrate inclusion, and act with kindness. We will all be judged. We can't avoid that in life. And everyone yearns to be accepted, so let's start as early as we can as parents and mentors, and set beautiful examples.

I am blessed to be a mother of four, be supported by a myriad of lifelong friends, straight, gay, transgender, and non-binary, and my life is full and rich because of every single unique soul. Remember, "diversity is a fact and inclusion is a choice." Make the choice to be inclusive and see the joy of your act.

Vanessa Williams

Actress on Broadway, television, and film, best-selling author, and multi-platinum recording artist. Recipient of the Human Rights Campaign "Ally for Equality" Award.

FOUR O'CLOCK!

Time for my big brother Noah to come home.

I had everything ready: flour, butter, sugar, and lots of sprinkles.

Not only is Noah the coolest brother, he is also the best cookie baker ever.

FLOUR

I waited for the hum of his skateboard,
his sparkly smile.

He always says, AWESOME, JOY! when he's proud of me.

But where was he?
There he was, racing with his boyfriend,
Miguel!

I was just about to call them, when Jimmy Dufflewood came out of his house with his friends.

The other kids laughed.
Some of them said mean words
about gay people.

Noah held Miguel's hand.

My chest started thumping.
My belly felt sick, half angry and half scared.
I wanted to scream at the bullies, but they were much bigger than me.

Miguel took off for his house.
Noah rushed to his room.

I didn't feel like baking now.
I just wanted to help my brother.

At bedtime, I told Mom what I saw and how I felt.

"It's not fair for anyone to treat Noah that way," Mom said. "I'm glad you told me about it, Joy."

"But what can I do, Mom? I want to help!"

"Of course you do!" Mom said. "It sounds like you want to be an ally."

"What's an ally?"

"An ally is a friend. Someone who stands up for people. Allies support others with words and actions. They might raise money for groups or places, like Noah and Miguel's Teen Center."

"But how can I raise money?"   "Well," Mom said, "you love to bake!"

The next morning at school, I grabbed my best friend, Elliott.

I told him what happened to Noah and Miguel, and about being an ally.

"Okay, I'll be an ally too," Elliott said.
"But we're just kids. What can we do?"

"We can have a cookie sale! We'll make
a bunch of money and give it to Noah
and Miguel's Teen Center!"

"But I can't bake," Elliott said.

"I'll teach you! Noah taught me."

We gathered a team of allies to bake on Friday after school.

Mom and I were in charge.

"Look, Noah! All the colors of the Progress Pride flag like the one in your room. **Hey! They're PRIDE AND JOY cookies! Get it?**"

Pretty clever, Joy!

Noah messed my hair.
But his smile wasn't as
sparkly as usual.

"Do you not want us to sell cookies?" I asked.
"Because if you don't, we won't."

"It's cool," he said.

Saturday was the big day. Dad helped me make a beautiful sign.

The cookie stand had the Progress Pride flag, the Ally flag, and more.

Before long, a line of people came to buy cookies.

A few more kids even joined our team.

Just as I was laughing with my ally buddies,
I heard a loud, mean voice across the yard.

NOBODY WANTS YOUR GROSS COOKIES AND YOUR GAY FLAGS!!

It was Jimmy.

My chest started thumping.
My belly felt sick again,
half angry and half scared.

But I'm an ally, right? What would an ally say?

I took a big breath.

"Listen, Jimmy," I said.
"No one gets to tell anyone
they don't belong, anywhere.

Everybody belongs here—
eating Pride and Joy cookies."

I put my arm around Elliott's shoulder. Elliott put his arm around the next ally, who put their arm around the next.

Soon, we made one long chain of allies.

WHATEVER!!

Jimmy stomped away.

My heart was still thumping. But I shrugged.

"I guess not everyone wants to be an ally."

"All we can do is try and not give up, right?" Mom said.

Just then, we heard a new voice.

"I want to thank you all.

There are still people who think folks like me don't belong.

But with allies like you, it's getting better.

Now, how about a dozen Pride and Joy cookies?"

Soon, we were SOLD OUT!

"So, what do we do now?" Elliott asked, jumping up and down.

"We keep on being super-duper allies! We stand up to bullies and include everyone. But for now..." I pulled out a special tray.

"We party! Who wants a cookie?"

"We do!" yelled the allies.

"We do too!' shouted Noah and Miguel and all the kids from the Teen Center.

Note to Grown Up Allies

Pride and Joy was written to assist children in understanding what it means to be an ally to people and groups they are not a part of—specifically the LGBTQIA+ community. Presenting allyship to children early in their development and helping them understand what it means to *be* an ally may reduce bullying and decrease homophobia and transphobia. Learning about allyship fosters inclusion, teaches empathy, acknowledges and celebrates diversity, contributes to a shift toward equality for all, and addresses heteronormativity with the goal of normalizing being LGBTQIA+.

It is often said that the word *ally* is a verb as well as a noun, and just as there are numerous conversations regarding allyship, there are also many ways to *be* an ally. In our story, Joy displays allyship by using her voice to stand up to a bully and by raising money and awareness with her Pride and Joy cookies. Here are some other ways you can foster allyship in children:

Allyship begins with you—You are a role model for children. They watch your behavior and listen to what you say. Begin by taking a look inside yourself and confronting any of your own biases and prejudices. Be willing to open up conversations and to listen. Reading our book with a child is an opportunity to answer questions and explore thoughts and feelings that may arise.

Keep learning—There are a numerous books available for children, teens, and adults that can serve as excellent resources and conversation starters to teach children about LGBTQIA+ topics, such as:

- What does Pride mean?
- What is Pride month, when does it happen, and why does it matter?
- Discover LGBTQIA+ heroes such as Harvey Milk, Mark Bingham, Ma Rainey, and Marsha P. Johnson, among many others.
- Learn about LGBTQIA+ history, such as the genesis of the Pride flag, the Stonewall Riots, and the AIDS Quilt.
- Discuss prominent straight allies in your community, in the media, and in sports.
- Talk about ally organizations and what they do for the LGBTQIA+ community.
- Teach children about language and pronouns.

Remember, when you don't know something, it's okay to ask!

Be respectful to the community—Being an ally is about respecting the voice of the group or community, not usurping it. In our story, Joy asks her brother Noah if it is okay for her to sell cookies for his Teen Center. Help children learn when it acceptable to offer help.

Show support—Join in Pride celebrations and festivities. Participation is important, but showing support is more than carrying an I'M AN ALLY sign or wearing a Pride pin. Support also comes in words: standing up for the rights of LGBTQIA+ individuals; speaking out about discrimination; and putting a stop to jokes, anti-LGBTQIA+ comments, and microaggressions. In our story, Joy raises money for a cause that is important to LGBTQIA+ people. Raising money and donating to organizations or groups who support LGBTQIA+ rights is a wonderful way of putting allyship into action.

Be an intersectional ally—People of color who are LGBTQIA+ face additional challenges in their lives. They may have to contend with racism, oppression, and discrimination that white individuals do not have to deal with. Talk to your children about these challenges, and invite them to think about how their words and behaviors can make a positive impact. Being an intersectional ally may also call you to discuss and acknowledge privilege with your children and how it may shape their experiences, thoughts, and behaviors. Privilege may be uncomfortable to talk about, but if we do not discuss the issues openly, we cannot find solutions to problems.

Be inclusive—This book focuses on a gay character, but the LGBTQIA+ community includes more than just gay individuals. Teach children about diversity in the community. Explain that the acronym LGBTQIA+ stands for Lesbian, Gay, Bisexual, Transgender, Queer or Questioning, Intersex, Asexual or Ally. The plus sign may mean pansexual, non-binary, two-spirit and others. It is important that children be an ally not just to one group of people, but to all. Use the flags as examples of the diversity within the LGBTQIA+ community.

Be humble—Learning and understanding aspects of a group you are not part of can be overwhelming, and you are bound to make mistakes. Often, people can misgender someone or use the wrong pronouns. Teach children to be kind to themselves, to be open to feedback, and to take action by being more conscientious next time.

Allyship is ongoing and genuine—Being an ally is not a "one and done" situation. Allyship begins with you and then spreads to the community. Change takes time, so it is important to stay the course. Allyship is not a fad or a trend, nor should it be performative. A performative ally is someone who acts like an ally to a group for reasons other than caring for a particular community or cause. They often act as allies to receive praise, recognition, or followers on social media. Teach children that this kind of ally is not consistent in their support, and that a true ally stays true to the cause even when no one is watching.

Seeking professional help—A book should never replace treatments such as psychotherapy or parent counseling. If your child is struggling emotionally or behaviorally at home, school, or other settings, or if you find yourself needing additional support, it may be appropriate to seek a consultation from a licensed psychologist or other licensed mental health professional.

All journeys are unique. There are many paths to take when it comes to being an ally! We hope our book provides a forum for discussion, educates children about allyship, and creates a sense of agency for children and the adults in their lives. We wish you and your children well on the road toward allyship!

Frank J. Sileo, PhD

Pride and Joy Discussion Questions

To get the conversation about allyship going, we recommend you consider some questions or points of discussion before, during, and after reading this book. Please use the questions that feel right for you and your child.

BEFORE READING

- In this book, you are going to learn what an ally is. Ally can be another word for friend. What are the important things about being a friend?
- What does it mean to stand up to someone or for something you believe in?
- Have you ever been bullied? What might you do if you see someone getting bullied?

DURING READING

- What does the word *gay* mean? Do you know anyone who is gay at school, among your friends, or in your family?
- How do you think Noah felt when Jimmy and the other kids made fun of him and Miguel because they are gay?
- Discuss what the word *Pride* means to the LGBTQIA+ community.

AFTER READING

- What is something you learned from the story?
- Are you an ally to kids who are in a group or community different from yours?
- What is something you can do to be an ally to someone?
- What do you do when kids are not kind to others?
- Do you have any other questions about the story?

GENDER HEROES

25 Amazing Transgender, Non-Binary and Genderqueer Trailblazers from Past and Present!
Illustrated by Filipa Namarado
ISBN 978 1 83997 325 3
eISBN 978 1 83997 326 0

THE BIG BOOK OF PRIDE FLAGS

Illustrated by Jem Milton
ISBN 978 1 83997 258 4
eISBN 978 1 83997 259 1

RAINBOW VILLAGE

A Story to Help Children Celebrate Diversity
Emmi Smid
Illustrated by Emmi Smid
ISBN 978 1 78592 248 0
eISBN 978 1 78450 533 2

Frank J. Sileo, PhD (he/him) is a licensed psychologist, international speaker, and award-winning author of 14 other children's picture books. He also wrote an award-winning parenting book that deals with raising chronically ill children. Since 2010, he has been consistently recognized as one of New Jersey's top kids' doctors. For over 27 years, he has worked therapeutically with LGBTQIA+ youth, adults, and families. Dr. Sileo has had his research published in psychological journals and is often the "go to" psychologist in the media. He lives in New Jersey and is an avid I Love Lucy collector. Visit drfranksileo.com and on Facebook, Twitter, and Instagram @DrFrankSileo.

Kate Lum-Potvin (she/her) is the multi-award-winning author of five picture books, including *What! Cried Granny* and *Princesses Are Not Quitters*. She lives in a Victorian house by the sea in the Canadian Maritimes with a musician husband and a mischievous Airedale. Her professionally produced stories and songs for kids can be found at kateandfriends.ca and on all podcast platforms. Follow Kate on Instagram at katelumpotvin_writer or visit katelum.com.

Emmi Smid (she/her) is a children's book author, illustrator, and translator from the Netherlands. Creating and translating children's books in her own cozy studio is what she loves doing most. When writing and illustrating, Emmi finds it important to pay attention to matters of diversity, inclusivity and mental/emotional well-being. Why? Because we're all unique, and we're not that different: we all want to be seen and heard and loved for who we are! Emmi's books include *Luna's Red Hat* and *Rainbow Village*. For all her books and illustrations, visit www.emmismid.com or her Instagram page.